THE MARE'S TALE

PET VET

Book #1 CRANKY PAWS
Book #2 THE MARE'S TALE
Book #3 MOTORBIKE BOB
Book #4 THE PYTHON PROBLEM
Book #5 THE KITTEN'S TALE
Book #6 THE PUP'S TALE

First American Edition 2009
by Kane/Miller Book Publishers, Inc.
La Jolla, California

First published by Scholastic Australia in 2008.
Text copyright © Sally and Darrel Odgers, 2008.
Illustrations copyright © Janine Dawson, 2008.
Cover copyright © Scholastic, 2008.
Cover design by Natalie Winter.

For information contact:
Kane Miller, A Division of EDC Publishing
P.O. Box 470663
Tulsa, OK 74147-0663
www.kanemiller.com
www.edcpub.com
www.usbornebooksandmore.com

Library of Congress Control Number: 2008933431
Printed and bound in the United States of America
17 18 19 20
ISBN: 978-1-935279-02-0

THE MARE'S TALE

Darrel & Sally Odgers

Illustrated By Janine Dawson

Kane Miller
A DIVISION OF EDC PUBLISHING

welcome to Pet vet clinic!

My name is Trump, and Pet Vet
Clinic is where I live and work.

At Pet Vet, Dr. Jeanie looks after
sick or hurt animals from the town
of Cowfork as well as the animals
that live at nearby farms and stables.

I live with Dr. Jeanie in Cowfork
House, which is attached to the
clinic. Smaller animals come to Pet

Vet for treatment. If they are very sick, or if they need operations, they stay for a day or more in the hospital ward which is at the clinic.

In the morning, Dr. Jeanie drives out on her rounds, visiting farm animals that are too big to be brought to the clinic. We see the smaller patients in the afternoons.

It's hard work, but we love it. Dr. Jeanie says that helping animals and their people is the best job in the world.

Staff at the Pet Vet Clinic

Dr. Jeanie: The vet who lives at Cowfork House and runs Pet Vet Clinic.

Trump: Me! Dr. Jeanie's Animal Liaison Officer, and a Jack Russell terrier.

Davie Raymond: The Saturday helper.

Other Important Characters

Dr. Max: Dr. Jeanie's grandfather. The retired owner of Pet Vet Clinic.

Major Higgins: The visiting cat. If he doesn't know something, he can soon find out.

Whiskey: Dr. Max's cockatoo.

Patients

Helen of Troy: A mare who is going to have a foal.

Paris: A Dalmatian dog who is Helen's best friend.

Map of Pet Vet Clinic

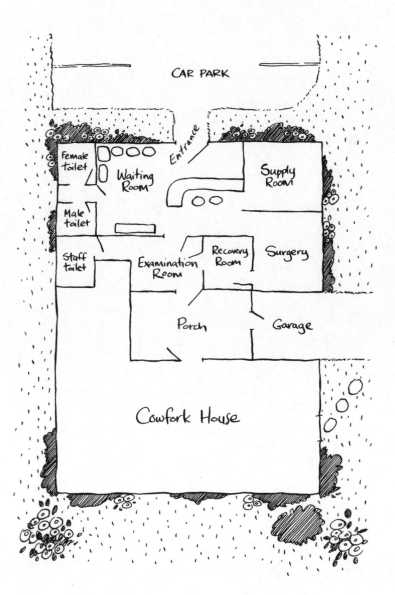

Morning at Pet Vet Clinic

It was a noisy night at Cowfork House. The rain poured and the wind blew. Every so often, a small branch would crack and I'd hear the rustle and crunch as it hit the ground. It was so noisy that I didn't hear the midnight train go through from Doggeroo Station.

I curled up under my blanket and listened to Whiskey shuffling his wings from his perch on the chair. Every time a branch cracked, he'd stick his crest up and mutter under his breath. Sometimes he'd mutter in Cockatoo-speak, and sometimes in People-talk that I'd better not repeat.

Whiskey and Dr. Max had come to supper, and stayed the night because of the storm. Dr. Max said the damp weather made his **arthritis** worse.

> **Arthritis**
> (arth-RI-tis) –
> A condition that makes someone's joints ache.

The alarm clock went off at six o'clock. Whiskey flapped his wings and squawked.

"Why do you *do* that?" I asked.

"A bird's gotta do what a bird's gotta do," said Whiskey. "It is a

cockatoo's duty to tell the sun to get up."

> **Cockatoo** (COCK-a-too) – Any parrot that has a crest of feathers on its head.

"There's no sun today," I said. "And that means no Major Higgins either. He hates the rain."

"Most cats hate rain," remarked Whiskey.

"Besides," I said, "we have a kitten with **cat flu** in the hospital. Higgins won't want to catch it."

> **Cat flu** – An infectious disease that makes cats very ill.

"Is he a cat or a chicken?" demanded Whiskey.

"If it was **beak and feather**

disease, *you'd* be chicken," I
pointed out. I let myself out in the
garden to do what dogs do, and
sniff-sniffed
around.

I pricked
up my ears
to listen for
Distress Calls
from animals

> **Beak and feather
> disease** – A
> condition where
> a cockatoo's beak
> and feathers
> break easily.

around the town, but all I could hear
was the storm. I ran back inside.

Dr. Jeanie was eating porridge in the
kitchen. She gave me a bit, too. When
we'd polished our bowls, we went out
to the hospital cages. Sometimes we
have lots of patients in the hospital,
sometimes we have hardly any. This
morning, we had two.

Harry Squawkalot was a parrot
who had broken his leg. Some birds
can manage with only one leg, but
parrots and cockatoos often perch
on one and use the other to hold
their food. Dr. Jeanie had set the

broken bone using a fine plaster bandage.

"He can go home in a day or so," said Dr. Jeanie, offering Harry a piece of apple. Harry took the apple in the claw of the bandaged leg and nibbled at it. That was a good sign.

The other hospital patient was the kitten. She was in **isolation**, so she wouldn't give her disease to

Isolation (I-so-LAY-shn) – Being on your own. An animal in isolation is kept away from others that might catch its disease.

other cats that came to Pet Vet Clinic. I followed Dr. Jeanie into the isolation ward and stood back while she checked the kitten.

"How are you feeling?" I asked.

"Sick!" said the kitten, and spat. "Go away, dog!"

I moved a bit closer and she hooked at me with her claws. I wagged my tail, because I knew she was feeling better. When she had come in to the hospital she had been far too sick to be rude to me. Part of my job as A.L.O. is to keep the patients from getting bored and depressed. If they like me, it's easy. I cheer them up. If they don't like me, they squawk or yowl or snarl at me. That makes them feel better, so my job gets done either way.

Dr. Jeanie scrubbed her hands and changed her coat. We have to be careful not to pass any disease from patient to patient.

It was still blowing a gale as we set out on Rounds at half past eight. We left Dr. Max behind to answer the telephone in the clinic. He was still grumbling about his arthritis. Whiskey stayed with him, clutching a milk arrowroot biscuit in one claw. I hoped he wouldn't eat all the biscuits before we came back.

Dr. Jeanie looked up the list of places we had to visit. "There are sick **calves** at Buttermilk Farm, then we need to see a new **mare** at Hobson's Stables," she told me. "After that, it's off to Jeandabah Run

Calves – Young cows.

to look at some sheep."

"Great!" I said, and

> **Mare** – Female horse more than three years old.

wagged my tail. I ran to the door to show Dr. Jeanie we should get started. We had to be back at lunchtime to open the clinic.

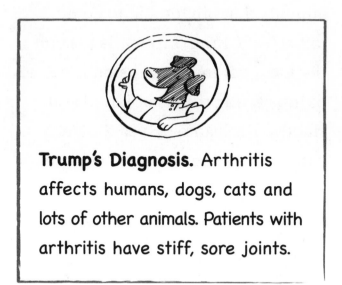

Trump's Diagnosis. Arthritis affects humans, dogs, cats and lots of other animals. Patients with arthritis have stiff, sore joints.

ROUNDS

When we do Rounds, we treat
animals that are too big to come
to Pet Vet Clinic. I like this part of
the job. I get to see and smell lots
of interesting things at farms and
stables. Dr. Jeanie drives the Pet Vet
van, and I sit on the seat beside her.
I wear a special harness that acts
like a seatbelt does for a human.
Dr. Jeanie says she has enough sick
animals to treat without having to
mend a broken Trump!

On this day I was glad I had my harness, as we had to stop suddenly when small branches blew out of trees and skidded across the road.

"What a day!" said Dr. Jeanie as we got to Buttermilk Farm. There were puddles all over the yard, and some of the cows were huddled under the hedges. Cows don't mind rain, but they hate storms.

Dr. Jeanie drove the van into the open end of the big barn. She put on her rubber boots and coat, and opened the van door so I could jump out. The farmer was waiting for us in the barn with two border collies.

"Flynn, Pammie, wait here!" said the farmer, and he and Dr. Jeanie went off to examine the sick calves.

"Stay, Trump," said Dr. Jeanie. "There won't be much room in the calf shed."

I stopped to liaise with the dogs. Flynn had been working as a cattle dog at Buttermilk Farm for a long time. The other dog, Pammie, was new. I stood next to the van and waited for Flynn to come over.

He came towards me slowly, wagging his tail, and we sniffed one another. "Hello, Trump," he said.

I wagged my tail. It pays to be polite when you're visiting another dog's territory. The junior dog came forward slowly, with her tail held low. We touched noses, and she started to roll over. This is called *submitting*.

"Get up, Pammie!" said Flynn. "Trump is a visitor. This is *our* territory, so you don't need to submit to her."

"Is that right?" Pammie asked me.

"Perfectly right," I said. "You don't submit to me because this is your territory, and I don't submit to you, because I am older than you. We are polite and friendly equals.

Flynn is top dog at Buttermilk Farm.
If you came to Pet Vet Clinic, *I*
would be top dog."

"She smells funny," said the
younger dog to Flynn.

"That's because she travels with
Dr. Jeanie," said Flynn. "Dr. Jeanie
is a vet, and some of the medicine
she has in the van smells funny."
He turned to me. "Pammie is my
apprentice," he said. "I'm teaching
her all the things a good cattle dog
needs to know." He sighed. "I think
I have a lot of teaching still to do."

Pammie jumped up and pointed
her nose outside the barn. "Should
we go with Master, Flynn?"

"Master said to stay here,"
reminded Flynn.

"But Master is going to the calves. It's our job to round them up and take them to the next paddock."

"Master said to stay *here*," said Flynn.

"The calves are sick," I reminded Pammie. "Dr. Jeanie will give them medicine to make them well. They need to stay in a warm place until they're better."

Pammie looked worried, but she trotted behind Flynn and me as we went further into the barn. We sniffed around the hay bales for a while and exchanged insults with one of the barn cats. That is, *I* exchanged insults with it. The only language Flynn and Pammie can talk is Dog-speak, although

they do understand some Human.
They had no idea what the barn cat
was saying to them, and that was
probably just as well. Would *you*
like it if a cat told you your nose
was dripping and your whiskers
were about to drop off?

"I hope you get cat flu," added
the cat.

"Don't be ridiculous," I said.
"Dogs can't catch cat flu."

The cat nearly fell off the hay
bales. "Yowwwwfitchhh! You *talk*!"

"So do you," I pointed out.

The cat's big eyes shone like
moons. "You talk Cat-speak! I
thought you were a dog!"

"I am a dog," I said. "I'm a terrier."

"You must be a cat. Only cats can

speak Cat-speak."

I yawned, showing the cat my fangs. "I'm a dog," I said. "I learned Cat-speak from a cat named Major Higgins."

The cat's eyes got even bigger. "Major Higgins is a legend! You're so lucky, dog."

Pammie scratched her ear with her hind paw. "What are you doing, Trump? Can't you talk properly? I can't understand you."

Flynn put his paw on Pammie's head. "Don't be silly, Pammie. Trump is talking to the cat."

"Dogs can't talk to cats," objected Pammie. "Cats just hiss and squawl."

"Trump can talk all kinds of languages. She can even talk to cows."

Just then, we heard Dr. Jeanie coming back.

Dr. Jeanie smelled of soap and disinfectant, so I knew she'd been washing her hands. Cat flu isn't the only sickness that can be passed from one patient to another.

Trump's Diagnosis. Submitting is what we dogs do when we meet someone who is higher up the pack than we are. It shows that the junior dog is going to be obedient. Kind senior dogs are nice to junior dogs that submit. That's why junior dogs do it.

Helen and Paris

"We need to see the mare at Hobson's Stables now," said Dr. Jeanie as she backed the Pet Vet van out of the Buttermilk Farm barn.

Rain splashed down over the windshield and poured over the windows. I pricked up my ears. I didn't know Hobson's Stables, so I thought this would be interesting. I love to go to new places.

Dr. Jeanie had to drive slowly, because the road was running with water. We were a good way out of town when we turned off into a driveway that ran between rows of hawthorn trees.

If it hadn't been so wet, Hobson's Stables would have looked neat and tidy. There were lots of square paddocks with white, painted fences. Each one had a shelter shed in one corner. When Dr. Jeanie stopped the van and opened the door, I smelled horses, but most of them were tucked away in their sheds, eating hay.

A young woman came out of the house. She had messy hair and her boots were too big. "You're the vet? Really?" She sounded surprised. A lot of people seem surprised when they meet Dr. Jeanie for the first time. Some people say Dr. Jeanie and I look rather alike. We are both tall and slim, with brown eyes. I am mostly white with a brown face and ears and a brown patch over my tail, and Dr. Jeanie often wears a white coat.

"Yes, I'm the vet," said Dr. Jeanie.

"I'm Shaz." She looked past Dr. Jeanie to me. "It might be best if you leave your dog in the van. Helen is nervous of small dogs."

"Trump is very good with other animals," said Dr. Jeanie. "Most of them like her. If your mare shows any uneasiness she'll go outside of her own accord." She reached down and rubbed my ears.

"She's not exactly my mare," said Shaz as we scurried towards the stable. "I'm in charge of the stables. The owners had to go away for a few days."

"I see," said Dr. Jeanie.

"I know all about horses," said Shaz. "I've done a course in horse-care. Only Helen is kind of special, and I'm worried. She's in the main stable."

The main stable was built of brick and had a proper door. Inside there were wooden partitions, with bales of hay and hessian bags full of some kind of grain. I sniff-sniffed the air. I detected the mare, hay, leather and something sweet, which I thought might be molasses. I also detected the scent of another dog.

I sniff-sniffed again. Hadn't Shaz said the mare was nervous of dogs? Did this mean a dog had been bothering her? Some dogs like to chase other animals. Mind you, some other animals like to chase dogs!

Dr. Jeanie and Shaz had gone into one of the stalls, so I shook the raindrops off my coat and followed.

A **bay** mare was lying down in a thick bed of straw. She turned her head, and Shaz rushed forward and grabbed hold of her halter. "Steady, Helen. It's all right."

Bay – A bay horse has a brown body with a black mane and tail and dark legs.

Shaz turned to Dr. Jeanie. "This is Helen of Troy. Mr. Hobson just got her a few months ago. She's really valuable. She's **in foal** to an Irish **thoroughbred**."

In foal – Going to have a foal.

Thoroughbred – A horse bred especially for racing.

"Hello, Helen." Dr. Jeanie moved forward to let the mare sniff her fingers, but Helen tossed her head sideways and rolled her eyes.

"Paris! Paris! I don't like this. There's a strange human here. There's a strange dog! Where are you?" Of course she used Horse-speak, but I knew what she meant.

"She is nervous, isn't she?" said Dr. Jeanie softly. "Is she always like this?"

"She's not too bad as long as Paris is around," said Shaz. "He keeps her calm."

"Is he another horse?" Dr. Jeanie asked.

Shaz laughed. "No, no, Paris is her dog."

"*Her* dog?"

"Her old Dalmatian," Shaz explained. "Racehorses sometimes have companion animals that travel to carnivals with them. I learned all about that in my horse-care course. They can be donkeys, or ponies, or even goats. Helen's companion is a dog. When Mr. Hobson bought

Helen, Paris came as part of the deal."

"Where is he?" Dr. Jeanie asked.

I had been wondering the same thing. It sounded as if Paris had a job, just like Flynn, Pammie and me. We didn't all have the *same* job, but we were all working dogs. If Helen needed Paris around he should be here. I sniff-sniffed. Had he gone to sleep in another stall?

"He's around somewhere," said Shaz. She yelled suddenly, "Paris? Parrr-isss! Here, boy!"

Helen swung her head up. Paris didn't come.

"He won't be far away," said Shaz. "As I said, Helen is in foal to an Irish **stallion**, and the foal will

be valuable
whether it's a
colt or a **filly**.
I wanted you
to have a look
at her today, so
she'll be used
to you when
the foal's born.
I can't afford
to have her
upset."

Stallion
(STAL-yon) – A male horse more than three years old.

Colt – A male horse less than three years old.

Filly – A female horse less than three years old.

I could hear Dr. Jeanie asking a lot
of questions about Helen and how
many foals she had had before, but I
was more concerned with Paris. If his
job was being a companion for Helen,
he should have come to see what Dr.
Jeanie and I were doing in her stall.

I soon found his trail, and followed it out to one of the other stalls. There was plenty of hay in there, too, and in one of the corners I found Paris. He was a big dog, and he was easy to see, because he was white with dark brown spots scattered all over his coat.

Since I was on Paris' territory, I approached politely with my tail in the visiting-dog position and waited for him to notice me.

He didn't jump up to challenge me, so I went a bit closer. He was asleep. I sniffed his paw. "Hey, you! Paris!"

He woke up with a jerk, and a tiny yelp. "Who are you?"

"I'm Trump, Dr. Jeanie's A.L.O.,"

I said. "You must be Paris, Helen's companion."

Paris tilted his head and peered at me. "You'll have to speak up, Crump. I'm a bit deaf."

"That's *Trump*," I said. "I'm named after a famous terrier." I repeated my explanation. "Dr. Jeanie is a vet," I added. "I am her Animal Liaison Officer."

Paris looked around and sniffed the air. I noticed his nose was dry. "I can't smell her," he said. Then he looked alarmed. "Did you say a vet is here? Is Helen all right? I should be with her."

"Yes, you should," I said. "She was calling you. I suppose you were having a nap."

"I must have been," said Paris. "I have lots of naps these days." He yawned, and I saw his teeth were worn.

"Come to her now!" I snapped.

I turned and trotted back to where Dr. Jeanie was examining Helen.

Trump's Diagnosis. Dalmatians are white when they are born, but when they grow up they have black or brown spots. This is different from Jack Russell terriers, which have patches as soon as they are born. Dalmatians are bigger than most terriers and they get along well with horses. Some Dalmatians are completely or partially deaf.

Chapter 4

Poor Paris

Helen hadn't calmed down when I reached her stall, so I went back to Paris, who was still where I had left him.

"Get *up*!" I snapped. "Helen needs you! Shaz is being silly."

"I want to get up," said Paris. "I tried, but I just can't. It hurts too much."

I came closer and gave him a nose-over. He didn't smell as if he was sick, but he didn't smell well either. "What is the problem?" I asked, much more gently. "Have you got a thorn in your paw? Or have you eaten bad meat?"

"No. I just hurt all over. I'm not as young as I was, and I often get tired. I don't mind that, but now I *hurt*."

I could see that he wasn't young. His eyes were not as bright as a young dog's would be, and his coat was dull. Now that I was thinking about him instead of about Helen, I saw he really didn't look well.

"Is that silly Shaz unkind to you?" I asked. "Does she hurt you? Does she starve you? She looks like the sort of person who might forget your food."

"Shaz is never unkind!" said Paris. "She's a little bit ... um ..."

"Silly?" I suggested.

Paris looked shocked. "Shaz is nice. She gives me beef and kibble, and I have hay to sleep in. She pats me sometimes. I can be with Helen all the time. I'm a lucky dog."

I thought hard. I'm not a vet, of course, but good A.L.O.s learn a lot from their vets. "Have you started feeling worse since this cold, wet weather began?" I asked.

"Much worse," said Paris. "But what am I going to do? I should be with Helen! Shaz is nice, but she's a little ... um ..."

"Leave it to me," I said. "I'm going to get Dr. Jeanie to help. She'll know what to do for you."

I trotted back to Dr. Jeanie. She

had finished checking Helen and was talking to Shaz.

"I think she'll have the foal quite soon, Shaz. It may even be tonight."

"Can you stay?" asked Shaz.

"Not now. We have to see some patients back at Pet Vet Clinic this afternoon, but give me a call if you're worried."

I was worried, so I went up to Helen and introduced myself. Helen was surprised to see me, and she wasn't pleased.

"Go away, strange dog. I want my Paris!" she said. "You make him come to me."

"Paris is not well," I said. "Dr. Jeanie is going to have a look at him."

"I want him here. I need him!"

"Calm down," I said. "You won't
help him or yourself if you go on
being so silly."

Helen stared at me and snorted.
"How dare you speak to me like
that, dog! Don't you know how
important I am? I have won races,
and I am worth a lot of money."

"You are just as important as any other horse, or any dog, and no more," I said. "Now be quiet! If you're going to have a foal soon you should keep calm. Otherwise, you will be too tired to look after it."

I left Helen to think about that, and went to Dr. Jeanie. She was still talking to Shaz, explaining just why we couldn't stay with Helen right now. I pawed her leg.

"Okay, Trump. We're going soon," she said.

I pawed again, harder, and yipped. When I had her attention, I darted out of the stall, then came back.

Dr. Jeanie understood that all right. "We'd better go and see what

Trump's found," she said to Shaz.

I led the way to the stall where Paris was lying. He lifted his head and flipped his tail a bit when he saw Shaz.

"There you are, Paris!" said Shaz loudly. "I thought you'd gone outside somewhere. What are you doing here, you silly dog?"

Dr. Jeanie crouched and held out her hand for Paris to sniff. "Hello, old fellow. Not feeling so well?"

"He's not all that old," said Shaz. "The people who bred Helen said he's about eleven. My aunt had a Chihuahua that was seventeen!"

Dr. Jeanie ran her hands over Paris. "Eleven is really quite old for a Dalmatian, Shaz. Did you realize he's **dehydrated**?"

"What?
But he can't
be! He has a
water bowl,

Dehydrated
(de-HIDE-rated) –
Dried out.

just outside the stable. I fill it with
fresh water every day or so ..." Shaz
sounded upset.

"He probably can't get to it easily
at present," said Dr. Jeanie. "He has
some arthritis in his back and legs.
You can see how stiff he is. He must
be in a lot of pain."

"But he's been all right. I mean,
he doesn't run around much, but
he's always pottering around where
Helen is."

Paris yelped as Dr. Jeanie felt his
hind leg.

"Poor old fellow, it hurts, doesn't it?" she said.

"Can you fix him?" asked Shaz. "I feel really bad that I didn't notice he was sick."

"It has probably been coming on gradually, and this bad weather would make him feel much worse," said Dr. Jeanie. "I can give him some medicine to make him more comfortable."

"Do you have it with you?" asked Shaz. "I could give it to him in his feed."

"I'd prefer to take him back to the hospital and give him a proper check up. If I can **hydrate** him, he'll feel a lot better, and then I can judge the right medication for him."

"Yes, yes … take him in, then," said Shaz. "Poor old Paris. I don't

> **Hydrate** (HIDE-rate) – Make wet, or give water to.

know what Helen is going to do though. They've been together since she was a filly."

"What's going on?" Paris asked me.

I realized he hadn't heard much of what was being said. Shaz talked loudly, but she also gabbled on a bit. "Dr. Jeanie is going to bring you back to Pet Vet Clinic and make you feel better," I told him. "You have arthritis. That means your joints don't move as well as they used to. That's why you hurt."

"I can't leave Helen," said Paris. "She needs me."

"You can't help her if you can't move," I said. "The sooner you feel better, the sooner you can come back to work." I crouched so my head was below Paris'. I wanted to remind him that this was his territory and that he was important.

Dr. Jeanie fetched a **thermal blanket** from

Thermal blanket – A special blanket that keeps body heat in.

the Pet Vet van and wrapped Paris in it. She settled him in the van. I slipped back to say goodbye to Helen.

"We'll be back to see you soon," I said. "Paris will come home as soon as he feels better."

Helen snorted, but I don't know if she was listening.

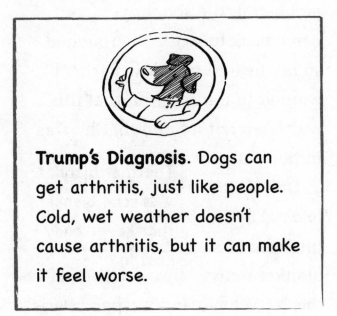

Trump's Diagnosis. Dogs can get arthritis, just like people. Cold, wet weather doesn't cause arthritis, but it can make it feel worse.

Back to the Clinic

We went to Jeandabah Run to check
the sheep, but I decided to stay
in the van to keep Paris company.
As A.L.O., I often have to make a
decision about who needs me most.
Besides, sheep respond best to
sheepdogs, like border collies. I am
not a sheepdog.

While we waited, I told Paris
about the clinic. He said he had
been there before, just after he came
to live at Hobson's Stables. Dr. Max

was running the practice then.

"I had a sore ear," he said. "Dr. Max put drops in it."

"You'll probably see Dr. Max today," I said. "And Whiskey. Do you remember him?"

"Of course," said Paris. "I couldn't forget Whiskey. He squawks so loudly even I could hear him."

"You weren't deaf when you were young, though, were you?" I asked.

"It's worse now, but I never did hear very well. A lot of Dalmatians are a bit deaf. One of my brothers couldn't hear anything at all."

This seemed terrible to me. We terriers use our ears a lot, although of course our noses are more important. I realized Paris was a humble sort of dog. Little things made him happy, and he loved to be needed. I suppose he had to be like that, to put up with Helen and Shaz.

When Dr. Jeanie finished with the sheep, we drove back to Pet Vet Clinic.

"It's nearly lunchtime," said Dr. Jeanie, "but I'd better get Paris settled first. You come too, Trump. He seems to like you."

The first thing Dr. Jeanie did for Paris was to make him up a warm bed with a heating pad. She also set up a drip. This is a kind of injection that puts liquid right into a dog's vein. It's really good for dogs who feel too sick or too sore to drink as much as they should. Sometimes medicine goes in with the drip.

Dr. Max came in to see Paris, and patted him. "I remember you, old friend," he said. "What's wrong now … arthritis?" He laughed. "Ouch. I know just how you feel."

"What does he mean?" Paris asked me.

"Dr. Max has arthritis too," I said. "Humans and dogs both get it. He takes medicine to make him feel better."

Dr. Max pointed to his ear. "I'm a bit deaf, too, Paris. So I *really* know how you feel."

"I'll see about some medication for him when he's off the drip," said Dr. Jeanie. "He'll feel better then." She sighed. "I wish we could cure him."

"That's the way it is," said Dr. Max, patting her shoulder. "Some things we cure, some things we treat, some things work and some don't. Let's have lunch, and then Whiskey and I had better go home to the Cottage."

We had lunch, and then it was time for the Clinic. I helped out where I could, welcoming patients and setting them at ease. Cordelia Applebloom brought my friend Dodger in with a sore paw. He had a big splinter and Dr. Jeanie had to get it out and disinfect the wound. We weren't surprised to see Dodger. Dodger is a very healthy border collie who is always having little accidents.

At the end of the Clinic, Dr. Jeanie cleaned up. Then we went to see to Paris and to feed the other hospital patients. The kitten told me to go away, but she ate a few mouthfuls of soft food. Harry Squawkalot flapped his wings at us and then got down to pecking up sunflower seeds.

Paris tried to get up, which wasn't easy with a drip attached to his leg.

"Lie down," I said. "You need to rest."

"I don't have time to rest," protested Paris. "I have to get back to Helen. She's the important one."

"*You* are important," I said. "And remember what I told you. The sooner you feel better, the sooner you can go home."

Dr. Jeanie gently pinched the skin on Paris' neck. "That's better!" she said. She disconnected the drip, and took it down. Then she gave Paris a small bowl of chicken soup and popped a tablet in his mouth. "You swallow that, and then go to sleep," she told him. "We'll see how you are in the morning."

It was dark by the time we left the clinic and went through the door into Cowfork House. Now that everyone had left, I noticed how noisy it still was. The rain rattled on the roof, and the wind hissed and whistled down the chimney and swished through the trees. I could hear small branches cracking and big ones creaking, and I wondered if Whiskey was asleep over in the Cottage where he lives with Dr. Max. Like most birds, Whiskey usually goes to sleep with the sun, but on a cold night like this he might be perched in Dr. Max's little kitchen.

Dr. Jeanie had lit the fire, so after supper, I stretched out on the fluffy mat and put my chin on my paws. Dr. Jeanie sat in the armchair, and closed her eyes. We were both tired. Despite the wind and rain, we went to sleep.

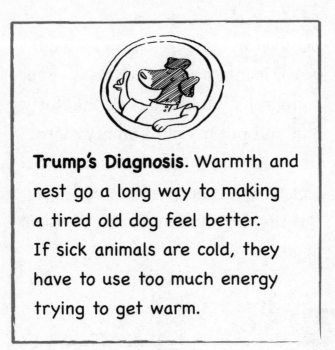

Trump's Diagnosis. Warmth and rest go a long way to making a tired old dog feel better. If sick animals are cold, they have to use too much energy trying to get warm.

Call in the Night

A few hours later, we woke up with a jump. The telephone was ringing. The fire was down to glowing coals.

Dr. Jeanie reached for the telephone. I wasn't surprised to hear that it was Shaz. She sounded wide awake, and I could hear her voice even over the wind.

"I'm sorry to disturb you on a night like this, Dr. Jeanie …"

"I suppose you want me to come and see Helen?" asked Dr. Jeanie.

"Well, yes. Nothing's wrong yet, but if something did go wrong it would take you a long time to get here in this weather. Can you come?"

Dr. Jeanie rolled her eyes at me, but she agreed to go and visit Helen.

It was still pouring with rain, and I was very cozy in front of the warm fireplace. I had to give myself a lecture.

"Trump, it is your duty as an A.L.O. to go with Dr. Jeanie," I told myself. "A pet dog could snooze in front of the fire all night, but you are not a pet dog. You have a responsible position."

Dr. Jeanie put on her coat and slung her sleeping bag and a blanket

into the Pet Vet van. Then she
turned on the answering service.
"Coming, Trump?" she said.

I looked at my basket, and then
at Dr. Jeanie. My basket was warm
and cozy. Dr. Jeanie wasn't ordering
me to come. It was up to me … of
course I was going!

Before we left, Dr. Jeanie looked
in on the hospital patients. Harry
Squawkalot and the kitten were
asleep, but Paris opened his eyes
and struggled to sit up.

"What's wrong? Where are you
going?"

"We're going to see Helen," I said.
"Everything will be all right."

"I have to go to her!"

I didn't have time to have this

conversation again, but I didn't want poor Paris to be upset. I reached through the cage bars and licked his face, just as if he were a sad puppy instead of a tired old dog.

"I'll tell her you're being sensible and getting better," I said. "That will make *her* feel better. I'm sure she's just as worried about you as you are about her."

I hoped so, anyway.

It took us quite a while to get to Hobson's Stables. The wind was blowing so hard we felt the van swaying as we drove along. I didn't like it, because the noise meant I couldn't hear things I usually take for granted. It was even difficult to hear Dr. Jeanie's voice.

The stable where Helen lived was lit up with electric lights, and the walls and roof were so thick the sound of the wind was muffled. I shook the noise out of my ears. I thought I should dry my wet paws and back, but I had only just started rolling in the hay when the fuss started.

Shaz came rushing out of Helen's stall. "I'm really sorry to bring you out on a night like this," she said again.

"That's all right," said Dr. Jeanie patiently. "How is she?"

Shaz pulled her coat around herself and twiddled with her hair. "She won't settle at all. She just keeps tramping around and around the stall. My horse-care course teacher said mares in foal should be kept calm."

"Have you tried tying her to the **manger**?" asked Dr. Jeanie.

"That makes her worse. I don't know

Manger – A trough for horses' food.

what to do!" Shaz's voice was high and I wished she would speak more quietly.

Dr. Jeanie dropped her sleeping bag and the blanket in a pile of hay and we went to Helen's stall.

Shaz was right. Helen was trampling around in her stall, muttering to herself in Horse-speak.

"Paris? I want Paris. Where's

Paris? It's not right. It's not good."

I sighed. I wanted to talk to
Helen, but the way she was
tromping around she might tread on
me by mistake. A flattened A.L.O.
is not much use, so I owed it to Dr.
Jeanie not to get squashed.

Dr. Jeanie watched Helen for a little while. "She's unsettled, but there doesn't seem to be anything actually wrong," she said. "I think the best plan is to turn out the lights and see what some peace and quiet will do."

"But then you won't know if she's all right!" said Shaz. She flapped her hands, and I thought she looked like a messy hen.

Dr. Jeanie smiled. "You go and get some rest, Shaz. Trump and I will stay with Helen. Don't worry. We'll look after her."

"But I can't just go to bed!" wailed Shaz.

"You should," said Dr. Jeanie. "You've already been up half the night."

It took a lot of persuading, but at last Shaz stopped flapping around and backed out of the stable.

Dr. Jeanie and I both sighed. Dr. Jeanie turned out most of the lights and spread out her sleeping bag. She kicked off her boots and settled down, and I crept under the blanket and settled beside her.

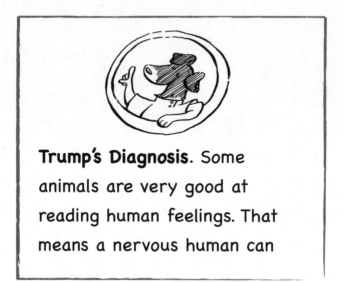

Trump's Diagnosis. Some animals are very good at reading human feelings. That means a nervous human can

make animals nervous. It
is better to speak in a low,
calm voice when you're with
animals. Of course, it's all right
to sound excited when you're
playing Fetch the Frisbee.

Chapter 7

In the Dark Stable

After Shaz left, I thought things would calm down in the stable, but Helen went on trampling around. I heard some rats squeaking in behind some hay bales, and again I had to give myself a lecture.

"Listen, Trump! Pet dogs can chase rats if they want. A responsible A.L.O. has more important things to think of."

I'd got that far with the lecture when I realized it was nonsense.

Chasing rats is an important job. Rats are noisy and they make food dirty. That means that the animals that eat it might get sick. It was my duty to keep those rats away from Helen.

I crawled out from under the rug and dashed across to the hay bales, yapping.

The rats squealed and chittered in Rat-speak. I could hear them in behind the hay.

"That's not the sad dog. That's a bad dog."

"It's not the spotty dog. Brother, can you see it?"

"It's a terrible terrier dog. Eeeeek!"

"A terrier dog? Terrier dogs chase rats."

"It can't get us. Rats are clever, rats are smart. Rats can out-rat any terrier."

The rats giggled, and one of them poked its nose out and whiffled at me. "Here, doggy, doggy!"

I bounced a couple of times. "Scat! Scat! Run, rat!" I yapped. "Scuttle off and don't come back!"

There was a tiny silence, and then a squeal, and a scuttering.

"It's a terrier that *talks*!" wailed the one that had whiffled. "*Eeeeeeeek*!"

"Scat, rat, scat!" I squeaked back.

After a moment, I heard them scuttling away until there was nothing left but their scent. That was wise of them.

"*Now* what?" said Dr. Jeanie.

"Rats! There were rats!" I scratched at the bales, just in case one of them was lingering. I snuffed loudly in all the cracks.

"Hush, Trump!" ordered Dr. Jeanie. "You'll upset the mare."

I cocked my ears. I could still hear the wind howling outside, but Helen had stopped trampling around. I trotted over to her stall and peeped in. She was standing in the corner, quivering.

"What is it?" I asked.

"Where's Paris? There are rats!" said Helen. "I heard them ratting around!"

"I chased them away," I said. "Remember I told you Paris wasn't well? I'm here instead."

"He's gone away! He's left me!"

"He's at Pet Vet Clinic," I said. "He's keeping warm and he'll soon feel better."

"Oh." Helen gave a small snort.

Since she had calmed down a bit, I moved closer. "Why not lie down yourself?" I said. "I'll stay and keep you company. The rats won't come back while I'm here."

Helen snorted again, and pawed at her bedding. "I'm going to have a foal," she said.

"I know," I said. "Dr. Jeanie is here too. She'll help you if you need her."

"Mfff." Helen lay down in the straw, then swung her head around so she could sniff at me. "I won a big race," she said suddenly. "Everyone cheered and yelled. My jockey said I was the best! It was so noisy."

"It's noisy tonight, too," I said.

"Different noise." Helen snorted again. "I won lots of races. Different races, different places. Not the same jockey. People cheering. Different people. But when I got back to my horsebox, Paris was there. Paris is quiet. He makes me peaceful."

"He'll be back," I said.

"You're not quiet. You're a noisy dog," said Helen.

"Only sometimes." I yawned. "I might be quiet when I'm an old dog like Paris. Only I can't be quiet if there are rats."

"I won a big trophy," said Helen.

"All those races. Now I'm here and I'm having a foal." Her voice had gone quiet, and she rested her nose in the bedding.

"Paris is old," I said. I wasn't sure if she realized that. Horses are smart, but they don't think like dogs. "If you are quiet and sensible he will be pleased. He'll be with you when he can."

"Hmfff." Helen closed her eyes.

I was dozing beside her when Dr. Jeanie crept into the stall. I opened one eye and flipped my tail to show her we were fine. The lights were on, and it seemed as bright as day.

Then I realized Helen had woken up. She was muttering to herself again, swishing her tail in the straw.

"Trump? Are you there?"

"I'm here. I said I'd stay with you," I said. "Everything is fine."

Dr. Jeanie stroked Helen's neck. "I thought so!" said Dr. Jeanie. "That foal's on its way. You'd better shift, Trump, in case she rolls on you by mistake."

I sighed, and put my nose back on my paws. I knew Helen wouldn't turn me into a pancake-A.L.O. She was used to sharing her stall with a dog.

"Everything is fine," I said again – but just then, there was a huge crack of thunder, and the lights went out.

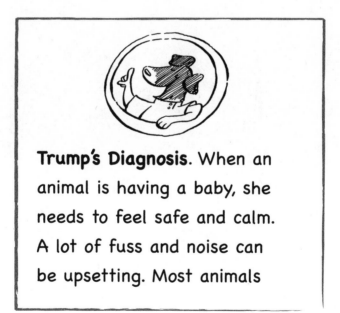

Trump's Diagnosis. When an animal is having a baby, she needs to feel safe and calm. A lot of fuss and noise can be upsetting. Most animals have their babies without any problems. Sometimes a vet helps make sure things go smoothly.

Chapter 8

Beginnings

"Bother!" said Dr. Jeanie. There was another growl of thunder and another loud crack.

Some dogs are really afraid of thunder, but I knew it was my duty to stay calm. I told Helen again that there was nothing to worry about. "The rats are gone, and thunder is only noise."

Dr. Jeanie can't see in the dark. I can see a bit, so I moved over to her and got up on my hind legs to nose her hand. Seeing isn't as important as smelling to me, but humans are different.

Dr. Jeanie waited a while, but the lights didn't come on. "I'll have to get the flashlight from the van," she said to me. "Wait here, Trump."

I heard her shuffle out through the straw, and then I could tell she was trying to find her coat and boots near the sleeping bag. It took a while.

I could hear Helen moving her hooves around. She got up, and shifted around in the stall, and then she lay down again. Now that she was really having her foal, she had stopped being silly. I moved back under the manger, so I wouldn't get trodden on by mistake.

"Mmfff!" said Helen. "Trump?"

"I'm here," I said.

"I feel funny. My foal is coming."

"That's very good," I said. "You'll like having a foal to look after."

"Mmfff." Helen grumbled a bit. I heard her breathing deeply. "It's hard work, having a foal," she said.

"You're strong," I said. "You're doing fine."

I heard a sort of slithering sound and then there was a thump and lots of snuffling. Helen whirled around so her tail flicked my nose, and I heard her mumbling to herself.

"Did it. Good. Hmmmmf." She sounded pleased.

The foal had been born! I heard

it moving around in the hay. It snuffled and sneezed, and Helen started to dry it with her tongue. That was a very good thing. Mother mares and cows are like mother dogs. We all lick our babies to dry them and to help them to start breathing properly. After a little while, the snuffling stopped, and I knew Helen was doing everything just right.

I was still under the manger when I saw light flitting over the straw and Dr. Jeanie came back into the stall.

"Well!" she said, and laughed softly as she shone the flashlight on Helen's baby. "Isn't that just like you, Helen? All that fuss and trouble and as soon as I go out you have your foal! May I have a look?"

Helen didn't take any notice. She was too busy talking to her new baby. Dr. Jeanie bent and made sure the foal was comfortable. Then she went out and fetched a rough towel. She helped Helen to dry and warm the foal.

Neither of them had much to say to me, but I felt happy. A new baby is always good to see, and I could tell that Helen knew how to look after this one. Paris would be pleased. I moved forward so I could have a good look. The foal was sitting up with its long legs folded. It had big ears that flapped a bit because Helen was still licking it. I could see a fuzzy little tail.

After a while, Dr. Jeanie sat back on her heels and watched as the foal managed to stagger to its feet. Helen nudged it into the right position with her nose. Soon it was having its first drink of milk.

"I should go and tell Shaz it's arrived safely," said Dr. Jeanie to me. Then she smiled. "Or maybe we'll wait a while. Shaz will fuss around and Helen needs some peace and quiet."

I thought that was a funny thing to say in a storm, but suddenly I realized the rain was much lighter now. There was no more thunder, and the wind had dropped. It really was rather peaceful.

Dr. Jeanie and I didn't get much sleep that night, but when morning came the sun was shining. Shaz came out and, sure enough, started fussing. "I had the alarm clock set but the power must have gone off and it didn't ring!"

"Everything is fine," said Dr. Jeanie. "Helen has a healthy filly foal. I'll come back to check on them later today. Paris will be well enough to come home, as long as you give him his medicine and make sure he's comfortable." She smiled. "Shaz, you might suggest to Mr. Hobson that Paris needs an apprentice. If Helen could make friends with a younger dog, Paris could rest more."

"I don't think Helen would like another dog," said Shaz. "She hates most dogs. She only likes Paris."

There was just one answer to that. I trotted up to Helen and licked her nose. Helen hmmmmfed and gave me a gentle nudge. I wagged my tail, and Helen nodded in a friendly way.

"Maybe Mr. Hobson could buy Trump!" said Shaz. "What a great idea!"

There was only one answer to that, too, and Dr. Jeanie gave it …

"I'm sorry," said Dr. Jeanie. "Trump has a job already."

About the Authors

Darrel and Sally Odgers live in
Tasmania with their Jack Russell
terriers, Tess, Trump, Jeanie and
Preacher, who compete to take
them for walks. They enjoy walks,
because that's when they plan their
stories. They toss ideas around and
pick the best. They are also the
authors of the popular *Jack Russell:
Dog Detective* series.

Also By Darrel anD Sally ODgers

JACK RUSSELL:
Dog Detective

Jack RusselL:
the detective with
a nose for crime.